TOBY DOG

of Gold Shaw Farm

By Morgan Gold

Illustrated by Xaio

Published in 2023 by Lillian Books
PO Box 225, Peacham, VT 05862

This book is a work of fiction. Any resemblance to actual dogs, cats, ducks, or skunks, especially those with an uncanny ability to steal your lunch when you're not looking, is purely coincidental.

For the dog who insists on digging up the garden—we still love you. For the cat who seems to think 3 AM is playtime – please reconsider. And for the duck who's mastered the art of quacking just when it's quiet—we hear you. But seriously, this is fiction. Any similarities are purely . . . quackcidental.

Printed in the United States of America

First Edition: September 2023

To Toby Dog. Your heart is as wide as the pastures you guard. This book is a testament to your quiet strength and the immeasurable warmth you bring. May your tail forever wag in the winds of our farm.

THE FARMER'S MAP
GOLD SHAW FARM

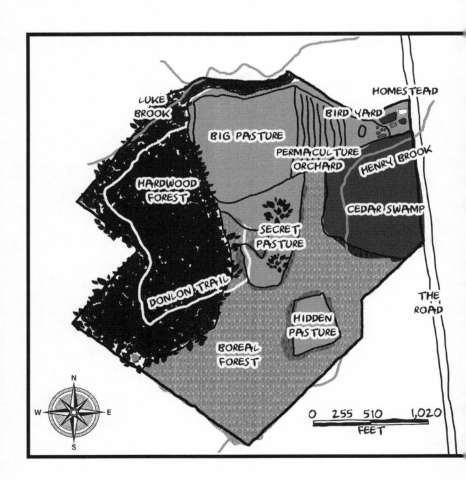

FOREWORD

by Jessica Sowards

My great longing for farm life was formed on the pages of a children's book. That book, a paperback picture book published in the 1970's, detailed the lives of a litter of kittens seeking their new homes. One kitten found home in a big red barn, and I vividly remember the way it marked my heart. I related. I, too, felt I belonged on a farm.

Morgan Gold is the best storyteller I know. I tell him this every opportunity I get, but I think it far more than I tell him. It is the characteristic that I would be quickest to use in description of him: Morgan, the excellent storyteller. It wasn't until quite a few years of friendship that I really realized what made the stories I'd heard him tell so very captivating, though.

It was winter, and Morgan came down to visit our farm on a trip he was making through the Southeast U.S. We'd had a great day milking cows, shooting content, and discussing our dreams and goals over lunch at the local diner. At the end of the visit, he downloaded some of the footage he'd captured of my farm and kids onto my computer for me to have. He'd put a camera on our dogs and on one of the chickens. I sat with my boys and laughed at the escapades of our animals. Then, we came upon a clip where Morgan had strapped the camera to my eight-year-old son, Ezra, and recorded Ezra running around the farm for five minutes.

When I watched it, I laughed and then I cried. There, in video format, was the first person-viewpoint of my curious, fierce son. There was the viewpoint of a childhood spent exploring a big red barn, the very thing I'd dreamed of since reading the book about the kittens when I was close to Ezra's age. I watched the clip over and over, climbing fences in Ezra's mind, running to the top of the dirt pile, and pausing to survey what he saw. That's when I realized, Morgan Gold is an excellent storyteller because he takes the time to value the experience of chickens and barn cats, of an eight-year-old farm kid and of a guardian puppy named Toby.

The stories of Toby Dog will be enjoyed for years to come for encouraging themes and valuable lessons. Through Toby Dog's eyes, we learn the value of bravery, of confidence in ourselves and of friendship despite differences. Surely, this story will plant a desire for a farm in the hearts of many young people. Even sweeter though, I believe it offers us all a chance to look at ordinary things, like a chewed garden hose, a little bit differently. If embraced, that gift of imagination could give us a whole new outlook on this wonderful world.

CHAPTER
🐾 1 🐾

The coyotes' howls echoed in the cold night air. The little white puppy with a black leather collar rolled over on his side, expecting to feel the warm body of his mother. But she was not there.

The little white puppy lifted his fluffy head and looked around the tiny three-sided shed, the only home he had ever known. His six brothers and sisters slept soundly in a snoring puppy pile. But where was his mother?

"Momma," the little white puppy whimpered. "Where are you?"

A deep, bellowing bark answered his question. He leapt to his feet and sprinted outside. It was a cold October night, and the moonlight felt as bright as the sun. The little white puppy's paws crunched on the cold, hard snow that had accumulated. Outlined in the light of the full moon, his mother stood, barking. For several minutes, her barks battled in a call-and-response with the howls of the hungry coyotes.

The little white puppy listened for a while, and then he joined his slight, high-pitched yelp to his mother's deep barks.

She turned to him. "What are you doing up, little one?"

"I'm helping," said the little white puppy.

She smiled and shook her head. "Oh, little one, you are fearless."

"Momma, why do we bark at the coyotes?" he asked.

"Because we need to protect the farm. Our kind is different from other dogs. For thousands of years, we have watched over our farms. I protect this farm, just like my parents protected their farms."

"Who are the bad guys, Momma?" asked the little white puppy.

"There are many. Coyotes, bears, raccoons, weasels, foxes. The list goes on. We must protect the animals on our farm from the wild animals that could hurt them."

"Will I guard our farm someday?"

"Someday, you will protect a farm of your very own," said his mother.

The coyotes howled again in the distance. The sounds took on a frantic and chaotic edge.

The little white puppy thought it was as scary as a thunderstorm.

His mother barked in response.

The little white puppy instinctually joined his mother. What his bark lacked in resonance, it made up for in speed. He got in two yips for every deep bark by his mother.

Finally, the coyotes quieted, their howls fading into the distance.

"Come to bed, little one. The coyotes are now miles away. We have done our job for the night."

They returned to the three-sided shelter. The little white puppy curled up between his still-slumbering brothers and sisters and his mother. Surrounded by warmth and comfort, he drifted back to sleep.

CHAPTER
🐾 2 🐾

"Cockadoodledoooooooooooo!" screamed the rooster as he broke the dawn's stillness.

The little white puppy woke to find that the little three-sided shelter that he shared with his mother, aunt, brothers, and sisters was empty. He was all alone.

The little white puppy was not afraid, though. He could hear his brothers and sisters playing in the farmyard. He got up and stumbled out of the shelter.

Warm hues of purple and orange tinted the sky. A light snow had fallen the night before, and the ground crackled with cold as he stepped on it.

The little white puppy's stomach grumbled. There was no doubt about it—he was hungry. Ever since his mother had stopped giving him milk last week, he found he was almost always hungry. But, as his mother told him, he was a big boy now—more than two months old—and that was too old for milk.

The little white puppy sniffed the air, hoping to detect a food smell. No luck. Just the smell of chickens, sheep, and the other dogs. These smells were the familiar smells of the little white puppy's farm. In fact, they were the only smells that he had ever known.

The little white puppy scampered toward the other puppies.

"Hey, puppy, I bet you can't catch me," wheezed a voice from behind him.

The little white puppy turned to see Barbara, his favorite chicken. She was an all-black chicken with a big fluffy poof of feathers on the top of her head.

The little white puppy forgot about his hunger, and he sprinted after Barbara, who waddled and flapped vigorously, trying to get away.

From the other side of the farmyard, the little white puppy's Auntie Ursula spotted him chasing Barbara. She barked loudly with the same loud and vicious bark that was usually reserved for coyotes, only this time it was meant for him. When it was directed at the coyotes, the little white puppy found the sound of her bark reassuring. Now it was terrifying.

He immediately stopped chasing Barbara and tucked his tail between his legs.

His aunt approached him. "We never chase the animals we protect," growled Ursula. "Ever."

"But, Auntie, I wasn't going to hurt her. We were just playing. Isn't that right, Barbara?"

He turned around to get confirmation from Barbara, but the chicken had rushed off to join the rest of her flock.

"I don't care if that chicken was wearing under-pants made out of dog kibble," scolded his aunt. "We never chase the animals we protect. You need to remember that. Soon, you won't have your mother or me to remind you."

"What do you mean?" asked the little white puppy.

"Never you mind," said Auntie Ursula. "You'll find out soon enough."

"Yes, ma'am," said the little white puppy.

The little white puppy slinked off to the corner of the farmyard that was farthest from the barn. He sulked under the old, bare oak tree. Feeling sorry for himself when things didn't go his way was something he did often.

The little white puppy spotted one of his sisters clomping toward him. He didn't know what her name was. In fact, he didn't even know what his own name was. None of the puppies had names. Their mother referred to them all as *darling*, *sweetie*, or *young one*.

His mother had a name—Francesca. His aunt had a name—Ursula. And all the chickens and sheep had names, too. But the puppies remained nameless.

The week before, one of the little white puppy's brothers had asked their mother why they didn't have names, and she told him they'd all get names once they got their own farms. The little white puppy couldn't quite understand what that meant. Didn't they already have their own farm? The little white puppy surely hoped that this farm was his own farm because he never wanted to leave. It was such a wonderful place. The little white puppy loved watching the chickens and the sheep. He loved to wrestle with his brothers and sisters. And he loved to sit quietly next to his mother as she licked his fluffy white coat of fur.

Because they had no names, the little white puppy and his siblings referred to one another by the color of the collar each one had wrapped around its neck. The little white puppy had three brothers: Yellow, Brown, and White. He also had three sisters: Pink, Orange, and Blue. And all his siblings called the little white puppy Black.

"Black, you messed up big time," said Pink, joining him under the old, bare oak tree, where he was sulking.

"I know," said the little white puppy.

"Well, the other puppies and I were talking, and

we think it's your fault we haven't been fed yet."

With Pink's words, the little white puppy's stomach grumbled with renewed intensity.

"The farmer lady came by earlier," said Pink. "And she took Brown and Blue with her. She hasn't been back since."

"She took Brown and Blue? What do you mean?"

"I mean, she took them! They're gone! She came with a man I have never seen before, and they took Brown and Blue. Mother followed them, but she came back a little later. That man smelled like the sheep."

"Where's Momma now?"

"I think she's over by the chickens."

The little white puppy ran off to find his mother. As he ran toward the chicken coop, Hezekiah, the ram, stopped him.

"Eh? Where do ya think you're going there, sonny boy?"

The little white puppy was in a hurry and didn't want to stop and talk. But the old gray ram was powerfully built. He had two large horns that wrapped around themselves in spirals on the sides of his head. And when he asked a question, the little white puppy thought it was best to answer. "I'm looking for my mother," he said.

"Trying to say one last farewell, eh?" asked Hezekiah.

"Farewell?"

"Aye. Today's moving day for all you pups."

"What's that mean?"

"Moving day, I say. Moving day. That's the day you puppies leave the farm and head to, to, well, I don't really know where for sure, but just not here."

The little white puppy sat on his haunches and looked at the old ram.

"Listen, sonny boy, I've been here on this farm for many seasons, and I have seen it happen year after year after year. Puppies are born, they spend a few months wreaking havoc with their big, clumsy paws and their little razor teeth, and then one day, *poof*, they all disappear. And for you and your lot, today is that day."

The little white puppy shuddered at the old ram's words. This farm was all he had ever known. He couldn't picture ever moving somewhere else.

"Pink told me that Brown and Blue are already gone."

"Ayuh. If I were you, I'd say my goodbyes to my mother and kin. If you don't act on it now, you might never get the chance."

Panicked, the little white puppy stuck his nose in the air and scanned for his mother's scent.

A slight breeze wafted in his direction, and the little white puppy detected his mother near the chicken coop.

He bounded over and found her perched atop her favorite boulder, the one that allowed her to survey the entire farm. She usually loved it on that boulder. But that day she looked sad.

"Momma, Hezekiah said that today is mooing day. What does that mean?"

"*Moving* day, little one. Moving day. The time has come for you dear puppies to get farms of your own."

14

The little white puppy didn't answer. He liked this farm.

His mother saw his worried look and kissed him. "It will be an adventure, little one. And you'll also get a name. Won't that be fun?"

The little white puppy thought about what his mother said. Getting a name of his own and a farm of his own did sound like fun, just like his mother said.

"Oh Momma, this is so exciting. Aren't you excited?"

"Yes, little one," said his mother as she turned away from him. Tears leaked from her eyes.

Suddenly, the little white puppy was struck by a thought. "Are you and Auntie Ursula and the other puppies coming to my farm?"

"No, little one."

The little white puppy's heart filled with dread. He didn't want to leave his family.

"This is just how it goes," his mother said. "Once you little ones get old enough, you must go to your own farm. It is what our kind has done for generations."

She gave him a friendly love nip. "Every animal on the farm has its own job. The chickens bring eggs. The sheep bring wool. The bees pollinate the plants and make honey. And we dogs protect the farm. Some big farms need lots of dogs. But this farm only needs one or two dogs to protect it. That means you puppies must find new farms."

A yelp sounded from across the farmyard. The little white puppy and his mother simultaneously cocked their heads in the direction of the cry.

From a distance, they could see the lady farmer carrying Yellow and White. Yellow whimpered and White barked.

"Momma, they are taking Yellow and White. We must stop them!"

"No, little one. That is not what we do. Your siblings must go. It is their time."

The little white puppy's eyes filled with tears. "This is horrible."

"You are growing up now. And growing up isn't always easy. But eventually you'll see it's for the best."

The little white puppy didn't feel like this was for the best. This felt like the worst. Just yesterday, he and his siblings had been laughing and playing in the barnyard and sleeping at their mother's side by night. Today they were being carted off, one or two at a time, to a mysterious and unknown fate.

The little white puppy's sadness quickly shifted to anger.

"I can't believe you are letting them take us!"

His mother wiped away his tears with her paw. She said nothing as she nuzzled her son.

The little white puppy's anger melted away. He huddled close to his mother and licked at her chin.

Lying next to his mother, the little white puppy must have dozed off at some point because the next thing he knew, he woke in the arms of the farmer lady. Confused and disoriented, he squirmed and whimpered, but the farmer lady only gripped him tighter in her large arms.

She carried him past the farm gate.

The little white puppy had never been out that

far before. For as long as he could remember, he had always lived within the fenced farmyard.

Outside the gate, a man in a gray hooded sweatshirt waited by a pickup truck.

The farmer lady carried the little white puppy toward him.

The man flashed a wide smile. "Hey, buddy. How's it going?" asked the man in a not-unfriendly tone of voice.

The little white puppy shook with fear.

The farmer lady handed the little white puppy over to the man's firm grip. "Here you go. He's all yours. Good luck."

"You seem a little nervous," said the man over the little white puppy's whimpering.

In the passenger seat of the pickup truck was a crate made of black wire. There was a blanket and a pillow in the crate. And a piece of something that looked like it would be good for chewing. The little white puppy wiggled his nose, sniffing. The man gently placed the little white puppy onto the soft blanket, gave his head a pat, and then locked the crate shut and slammed the truck door.

A few moments later, the truck's engine sputtered to life, and the little white puppy and the man rolled away from the farm.

CHAPTER
🐾 3 🐾

The gray pickup truck rolled to a stop, and the little white puppy snapped awake. How long had he been sleeping? He wasn't quite sure, but he was now wide awake and panicked. He tried to look up through the top of the crate, but the metal bars wouldn't let him peer through the truck's passenger-side window.

It was still daytime, that much the little white puppy could see.

The man, who smelled of sweat and peppermint, sat behind the steering wheel of the truck. "Easy, buddy. We're here," he said. "We're finally at the farm."

The farm? Was this farm going to be *the* farm? Was this farm going to be *his* farm? Did that mean that this man who had been driving him was a farmer?

The man got out of the truck, grabbed the crate, and placed it on the ground. "Welcome to our farm!"

The little white puppy looked through the wire wall of the crate. This farm reminded him of his home, but it also felt very different. The white farmhouse could use a layer of paint, or four, and it was dwarfed by an ancient three-story barn. The barn at his mother's farm was much smaller. And the little white puppy heard quacking and honking in the not-too-far distance.

But cats had been on Momma's farm. And cats were at this new farm, as well. Two tabby cats sat on the wraparound porch of the house. They eyed the little white puppy with suspicion.

"That is the weirdest-looking cow I have ever seen," said the smaller of the two cats.

"That's no cow," said the other one. "That's a dog. I've seen dogs before. They can be trouble."

The farmer opened the door of the crate, and the little white puppy scampered out. The hours-long truck ride had caught up with him—his bladder felt like it was an overfilled water balloon. He made his way over to a dormant rosebush near the porch and lifted his leg.

"The lack of manners in this creature is appalling," hissed the small cat.

"Now, Lil Barn Cat, don't be rude. He's had a long journey," said the farmer. "I think you're really gonna like it here, boy."

The farmer crouched down and scratched behind the little white puppy's ear. It felt good. The farmer had a very gentle touch.

"By the way, you need a name," said the farmer. "The paperwork I filled out with the breeder has you listed as Sir Bartleby de Mimsy-Porpington, Earl of Caledonia County, but I think we're just going to call you Toby Dog for short. What do you think?"

Toby Dog! The little white puppy liked the sound of that. It had a nice ring to it.

The farmer walked Toby toward a pen with a woven wire fence that sat on the south side of the barn. Inside the pen was a shelter that had a hay-covered floor and wooden slat walls.

The farmer opened the metal gate. Toby cautiously stepped into the pen.

"This is where you'll be staying," said the farmer. "I'll let you have time to get used to your surroundings, and I'll be back to check on you in a bit."

With an ear-cracking clang, the farmer closed the gate and headed back toward the house. Toby sniffed the air. This place smelled different from his mother's farm, but it still smelled like a farm. Across from his little yard was another yard that housed dozens of ducks, geese, and chickens. They made their loud clucks, quacks, and honks and paid little attention to him. While Toby was distracted watching the ducks, geese, and chickens, something snuck up on him. He felt a creature sniffing at his hind parts. Whipping around, he found the smaller of the two cats. He kindly returned a friendly greeting by sniffing her rear end. But before he could get more than two sniffs in, the cat slashed her paw and scratched Toby's nose.

Toby yelped! Tiny droplets of blood crept out of his nose.

Both cats darted several feet backward.

"Why did you do that?!" yelped Toby.

"Look here. My name is Lil Barn Cat, and his name is Pablo Barn Cat," said the small cat as she gestured toward the bigger cat. "This farm is ours, and we don't need some fluffy slobber machine messing anything up. You got that?"

"This is your farm? Oh, I thought it was going to be my farm," said Toby.

"Yeah, you definitely have that one wrong," said Lil Barn Cat.

Toby whimpered in confusion. He looked closely at the two approaching cats. Pablo Barn Cat was a thick and chunky tabby with piercing green eyes and a white belly. He moved with a confidence that suggested he was no stranger to scrapes and fights. The second one, Lil, was a smaller, more timid-looking tabby with fur that was more brown than orange. She kept close to Pablo, as if seeking protection. As they got closer, Toby Dog could see the hostility in their eyes. Their tails were puffed up and darted back and forth.

Toby backed away slowly.

"Well, I don't want to take your farm," sobbed Toby. "They took me away from Momma's farm and now I'm here and I'm scared and I miss my mother and my brothers and sisters and I don't know what's going to happen and the farmer guy seems nice, but maybe he's just pretending and I just want to go home!"

"Calm down, pal," said Pablo. "You're embarrassing yourself, as well as everyone else here. We might be able to make use of a dog here. But you're going to have to do what we say. OK?"

"OK," Toby said and nodded.

"Now, for starters, see that dog food over there?" said Pablo.

Toby turned his head in the direction of Pablo's pointing paw. His nose was immediately hit with the smell of food. YUMMY FOOD! With all the action of the day, Toby had forgotten that he hadn't eaten all day.

"We get first dibs on all the food on this farm," said Lil. "You can only eat after we're done. Understood?"

Toby nodded. He'd been so scared about the trip that he hadn't noticed how incredibly hungry he was. Now that the barn cats had made him aware of the food, he could feel the hunger twist his puppy belly into a tight knot.

Pablo and Lil sauntered over to the bowl and began to eat.

It looked like kibble with some chicken hearts. It smelled divine.

A few flecks of drool dribbled down his chin.

Toby couldn't stand to watch. He wandered over to the corner of his doggie shed, curled up in the pile of straw, and began thinking of a way to escape this place and go back to Momma's farm.

CHAPTER
🐾 4 🐾

That first night for Toby was a tough one. It was the first night he had ever spent alone. While he could hear the ducks chattering off in the distance, and the farmer came to visit him every few hours, there were lots of low points in that long, lonely night where he was just all by himself. Even the surly barn cats had abandoned him after eating all the chicken hearts out of his dish.

The little shelter that sat inside his yard was warm and cozy. The floor was covered in straw. There were some bones to chew and plenty of fresh drinking water. The temperature was warm for October in Northern New England . . . but he was alone.

One good thing about being alone was that while the barn cats had first dibs on his food, Toby found he could eat as much kibble as he wanted without competing with his brothers and sisters to get his fair share. And no one stole his bones. So he ate as much as he wanted, and he washed his meal down with cold water, and he spent quite a bit of time chewing on the lovely little bone that the farmer had given him. And when he felt like he had chewed all of his chews and played all of his plays and eaten as much as he could, Toby curled himself up in the shelter and went to sleep.

That first night, sleeping was quite comfortable until Toby was awakened in the middle of the night. The sound was a familiar one. It was the yipping and yelping of coyotes. But these weren't the coyotes from Momma's farm. They were different. He could tell there were more voices in the choir, yipping and yelping and chanting and screeching, and the accent they had was slightly different. He could hear them singing about some animal they were eating, perhaps a deer carcass they'd discovered—they were still too far away for Toby to make out their words.

Their yips were coming closer, though.

Even though he'd just arrived and he was already plotting his escape from this farm, instinct drove him out of his bed, and he began to bark. He barked as loud as he could.

And with each bark, the coyote shrieking momentarily stopped.

Toby sniffed the air. He could smell the coyotes, their musky, oily scent and foul, rotten breath. And he could hear them slowly padding along the pasture, slinking along the tree line. He could sense them. He knew they were out there, and although they weren't yelping, he could tell they were coming closer and closer.

Toby barked even louder. There was no way he would let coyotes invade his farm on his first night. But what would he do if the coyotes got close? He'd never had to fight a coyote before, let alone several coyotes, all by himself. Heck, he'd never even fought coyotes with help. He'd seen Momma and Auntie Ursula fight coyotes. That was as close as he'd ever come. The thought of fighting coyotes scared little Toby Dog, but it didn't stop him. He barked his meanest bark possible.

A coyote came up to the fence. He saw Toby and said, "Hey kid, what are you doing here? You're new. We usually come out here to look for stray ducks. We like ducks. We want to eat those ducks."

"We also like chickens, too," cackled another coyote standing farther back from the fence.

"Well, you're not going to eat those ducks while I'm around," said Toby.

"Kid, who are you kidding?" The coyote laughed. "You're just a little ball of fluff. There's nothing you can do to us to scare us off."

Although the coyote was taller than Toby, he was also skinnier. His mangy fur clung to his scrawny body. He was missing teeth, too.

Toby could tell just how underfed and malnourished this coyote was. He gave the loudest, meanest growl he could. The coyote jumped backward. From the shadows of the trees, the rest of the coyote pack emerged. Toby's heart beat so fast, it felt like it might explode.

"So that's how it's going to be, huh?" said a

large female coyote. "You're going to get your fight on with us, huh? We offer you friendship—a stepmother, even. But you're not going to hang out with us? You're not going to be friends with us? Be on the lookout there, kid, because we'll catch you in time. We're going to get past that there fence. We'll jump through that electric wire, and we'll get you. Mark my words, kiddo."

Although Toby was terrified, something inside him clicked into place. He went into what Auntie Ursula called "berserker mode." He barked and growled and snarled at those coyotes. He wasn't going to be intimidated. All the lessons he'd gathered by watching Momma for his entire life came flooding into his memory. He knew coyotes were not to be trusted.

As Toby continued to bark, the ducks and geese were awakened. Terrified quacks and honks filled the night.

"So now the farmer will come out, huh?" said the lead coyote. "Pack, let's go." She threw Toby an evil look. "Remember, kid. You chose this battle."

The coyotes retreated into the forest, leaving Toby Dog barking alone at the fence.

After a few minutes, Toby stopped barking and caught his breath. His heart was still racing. But it began to slow. And as it slowed, he thought about things. He was alone. He didn't have his mother or his brothers or his sisters or his aunt. It was up to him to protect this farm. It was his job. It was what he was meant to do. It wasn't going to be easy. But he would protect the farm or die trying.

Toby couldn't fall asleep until the wee hours of that morning. He just sat by the fence waiting and listening for yelps that would alert him to the returning coyotes.

As Toby remained on watch, Pablo Barn Cat and Lil Barn Cat watched him from a high rafter inside the old barn.

"Would you look at that?" said Lil Barn Cat. "The dumb floof ball has some guts."

"Yes," said Pablo Barn Cat. "He might be exactly what we need around here."

The barn cats continued to chat quietly with each other as the rest of the farm went back to sleep. Their voices were low and comfortable as they discussed the various goings-on of the farm. They talked about the new puppy, the state of the mice population, and the strange noises they sometimes heard coming from the old barn. As the night wore on, they eventually drifted off to sleep, their dreams filled with the endless possibilities of the next day's adventures.

Far above the sleeping barnyard, a female owl glided silently through the darkness, her wings barely stirring the air as she flew. Her feathers, a mottled mix of brown and white, were perfectly adapted for blending in with the trees and bushes of the forest. She had a sharp hooked beak and piercing yellow eyes that seemed to see everything. As she neared the old barn, she caught sight of a small mouse scurrying across the snow. Without hesitation, she swooped down and snatched the mouse up in her talons, a triumphant gleam in her eye.

As the owl flew off into the night, the farm animals snoozed. The only sounds were the soft rustling of the wind through the trees. It was as if the brief bloody encounter between the owl and the mouse had never happened. It had been just a momentary disturbance in the peaceful rhythm of the countryside. But Toby Dog, still awake and lying on the ice outside of his dog shed, knew that he had witnessed something special. He would never forget the fierce beauty of the owl as she flew away into the darkness.

CHAPTER
❖ 5 ❖

The following day, Toby awoke in his new straw bed. The surroundings still felt strange to him. The sheet metal roof of his shed seemed shiny and new compared with the rusted shed he grew up in. The structure was also spacious compared with the cramped but cozy home he had come from.

Late last night, the farmer had given him a deer hoof to gnaw on.

When he woke, Toby was hungry, so he went to town on that deer hoof, munching and gnawing away.

Shortly after sunrise, the farmer returned to

the shed. Toby sprang to his feet with his tail wagging wildly.

"Hey, Toby Dog," said the farmer. "How are you doing, buddy boy? How was your first night on the farm?"

The farmer scratched Toby behind his ear.

This thrilled Toby. He was even happier when the farmer produced a steel bowl filled with food. He devoured it in large, greedy gulps. Toby wasn't taking any chances with the barn cats roaming around.

"We've got a big day planned today," said the farmer. "I'm going to give you a tour of the farm, and you're going to get to meet your animals."

Toby's tail wagged even faster. Had the farmer just said that he would meet HIS animals today? This news was very exciting to Toby indeed. He had never had animals of his very own before.

The farmer attached a leash to Toby's black leather collar. Toby wasn't sure if he liked the leash. It was his first time wearing one, and the sensation felt weird.

"Don't worry, buddy," said the farmer. "You won't have to wear the leash often. Just until you get trained up around the farm."

He scratched behind Toby's ear again. "OK, come on, Toby Dog, come with me."

Toby bounded after the farmer, who walked toward the duck house.

"Now, Toby Dog, I know you come from a long line of livestock guardian dogs, and I know that your mother is an outstanding livestock guardian dog. But just to make sure we're perfectly clear, I want to take a few minutes and talk to you about the job of a livestock guardian dog."

Toby cocked his head, listening.

"There are four rules you have to follow. Number one, always protect your farm. Your job, your only job, is to make sure that your animals remain safe. In the woods surrounding our farm, there are countless predators—coyotes, bobcats, foxes, bears, owls. Any of these creatures could easily snatch a duck and find it to be a tasty meal. And, yes, we lock our animals up at night, and, yes, we have fences to help protect against animals coming into our farm and attacking our birds. But when it comes down to it, you, Toby Dog, are our true line of defense. Doing your job properly means you will save hundreds of bird lives. If you screw up your job, it could mean dead birds or even worse."

Although Toby Dog wondered what could be "even worse" than dead, this first rule made a lot of sense. He remembered the nights he heard his mother barking. Every time she barked, she was always barking at some animal.

"The second rule, Toby Dog, is that you don't fight. This farm is your farm. It is your territory. And I want you to protect and defend the territory. But there are ways to do that without fighting."

He looked at Toby to make sure he was listening. "If animals come close, bark them away. Walk the perimeter of your farm on a regular basis, marking your territory and declaring that this is Toby Dog's farm."

Toby stood up tall and gave a bark to show he understood.

"You know, there's a misconception that you livestock guardian dogs are typically good fighters, and I'd never want to tangle with one of you fellows if you saw me as a threat. But you livestock guardian dogs don't need to fight if you take the proper steps to ensure predators don't come over the fence. Yes, if an animal sneaks in, you must be ready to fight. But for the most part, your job is intimidation. Flash your big, pearly white teeth and give your deep, deep belly bark or your snarling snarl of a growl. Scare them! Yes, I know, Toby Dog, you have a very true and soft heart. But your job requires you to put on a mask and strike fear into the hearts of the animals that could harm your animals."

Toby tried awkwardly to snarl at the farmer.

"That's adorable, pal. But you can't snarl with your tongue hanging out," said the farmer as he scratched Toby Dog behind the ear.

"The third rule is don't leave your farm. If you

leave your farm, you are vacating your territory. You are leaving your farm unprotected. You are leaving your birds unprotected. You are inviting trouble and danger to come our way. I know our fence could easily let mischievous puppy dogs sneak through, but it's your job to resist that temptation. It's your job to stay here with your birds and keep them safe. Resist the urge to wander."

He took a breath and continued. "And finally, the fourth rule is never hurt your birds. Birds can be annoying, geese can be aggressive, and chickens can get up in your business. But you have to resist that urge to give them a comeuppance. I know they can sound an awful lot like squeaky toys, but you are not allowed to play with them. You are the one who has to take the high road."

He stopped and looked closely at the puppy. "Do these rules make sense for you, Toby Dog?"

Toby tried to say yes, but, unfortunately, he was unable to speak farmer. The noise he ended up making sounded like a yawning groan.

The farmer led Toby out of his paddock. Toby looked around. He was struck by the sights, smells, and sounds of the farm. His paddock and shed were directly across from a wooden building that sat on stilts. It was raised up two feet off the ground. The building was bigger than his shed—probably about the size of the garage where the farmer had parked his truck the night before.

"That right there is the duck house. All the ducks live there. The geese and the chickens are living in the barn for the winter."

The farmer opened a gate and led Toby into the paddock surrounding the wooden duck house.

Toby sniffed at the air. The acrid smell of duck poop, which smelled like a mixture of wet newspapers and old sneakers, filled the air. Muffled quacking came from the duck house.

"Are you ready to meet the ducks?" asked the farmer.

Toby gave an acknowledging wag of his tail.

The farmer walked up to a small door connected

to a ramp, unlatched the door, and swung it open. "RELEASE THE QUACKEN," he bellowed.

Ducks streamed out of the door and down the ramp. They waddled out, one after the other.

Toby noticed there were two breeds. Most were smaller and light brown in color, but there were also two white ducks that were much larger than the rest.

"The brown ones are the Khaki Campbell ducks. The big white ones are the Pekin ducks," said the farmer.

Once the ducks were all in the paddock, Toby counted twenty-nine of them.

"Toby, meet the ducks," the farmer said in an overly formal sort of way. "Ducks, meet Toby Dog. He's here to watch over you."

Toby wagged his tail eagerly and approached the ducks, who were huddled closely together. As he stepped forward, the closely bunched-together ducks scattered away from him, all quacking, flapping, and raising quite the ruckus.

"Yeah, it will take a little bit for the ducks to get used to you, Toby."

The farmer left the paddock and closed the gate, leaving Toby alone with the ducks.

The larger of the white Pekin ducks approached Toby.

"What are you? You don't look like a duck. And you don't look like a goose. You could be a chicken, but I'm not totally sure."

"My name is Toby. I'm the new guard dog at this farm."

"Guard dog, eh? And what are you supposed to guard against?"

"Uh, I guard against, uh, bad stuff, I guess."

"Bad stuff? Like what?" asked the curious white duck.

"Like big, scary foxes trying to steal the obnoxious chickens," snarked a brown drake with a sneer. "Or maybe he'll guard against the dangerous raccoons trying to get into the garbage cans. No, I know. He's going to guard against aliens trying to abduct the cows."

Nearly the entire flock of ducks burst into quacking laughter.

Toby Dog blushed.

He was mortified.

He tried his best to impress the ducks, wagging his tail and barking excitedly. But that only made them laugh harder! He couldn't believe it.

The duck flock quacked and chuckled, clearly enjoying his discomfort.

Toby turned and ran as fast as he could, his tail between his legs. There was nothing quite as humiliating as being laughed at by a bunch of ducks.

"Quit your quacking, you silly fools," said the biggest fluffy white duck. "I, for one, am pleased to hear that our farm has a new guardian and protector."

Toby noticed that the big, fluffy white ducks were not laughing.

"My name is Jemima Puddleduck," the big duck continued. "And this is my son, Samson," she said as she gestured toward the other white duck. "Say hello, Samson."

Jemima Puddleduck bowed in a formal curtsy.

"Nice to meet you," said Toby.

"My dearly departed husband, Samuel, was killed this past summer by a vicious monster. Having a fierce canine such as yourself could help our collective safety here on the farm."

"Ah, that puddleduck is crazy," said a brown drake duck with a white stripe on his neck. "Her husband probably went off to buy some milk and never returned."

The flock of brown ducks laughed.

"Yellow Neck, you take that back," said Samson Puddleduck, who was much bigger than the brown drake duck. "A monster killed my father. I saw it myself. It was a fierce creature ten times the size of one of the barn cats with eyes like red coals and gigantic claws the size of goose wings."

"Sure," chuckled Yellow Neck, the drake. "And I bet there is a magical creature that walks on two legs who comes and collects all the duck eggs every morning."

The flock of Khaki Campbell ducks burst into quacking laughter once again.

"Don't worry about them," said Jemima. "They're silly half-wits. We're glad to have you here, Toby. We need a good protector."

The farmer returned carrying large buckets of water. He dumped them into a blue plastic kiddie pool.

Even though there was snow and ice on the ground, the ducks quacked in approval. They hustled and bustled to the pool, pushing and shoving and stepping on toes, then dipping and diving and splashing about. They were very happy.

And Toby was happy, too—happy they were done making fun of him.

The farmer let him out of the paddock, and he decided to skedaddle away from the ducks and walk his farm.

Up by the barn, a flock of large gray geese waddled in front of Toby Dog. He was hesitant as he approached them. He'd spent his entire life at his mother's farm, and he'd never had the opportunity to explore beyond its boundaries. Now, as he stood in the snowy fields of his own farm in Vermont, he was overwhelmed by the sights, sounds, and smells that greeted him. The geese, with their regal bearing and distinctive gray and white feathers, seemed intimidating to him. He barked nervously and kept his distance, trying to gauge their reactions.

The geese, for their part, were not particularly pleased by Toby's presence. They hissed and fluttered their wings, trying to ward him off. Toby backed away, his tail between his legs.

Going the opposite direction from the geese, he set off sniffing and exploring the farm. The barn was to the east of the barnyard—all three stories of it hulking over the farm like a mother hen watching over her brood.

To the north of the yard were large expanses of pastureland. A small pond and more pasture occupied the western landscape. And roughly fifty yards beyond the south fence lay a large cedar forest. The farmyard was about the size of Momma's farm. Gosh, he missed Momma and Auntie Ursula and all his brothers and sisters.

Or maybe he just felt like he missed them so much because he was tired. And maybe that's also what made him feel so bad about the mean ducks and the stuck-up geese. After a full night of barking at coyotes, Toby was tuckered out. And everything feels harder when a fellow is tired.

He found a small hill that gave him a great view of the farmyard, and he lay down to rest.

Toby was having an exceptional dream of chewing on a rather large and enjoyable bone when suddenly he was wakened from his slumber by a sharp nip on his tail. He shot up and began to bark at the unseen attacker. Twisting around, he saw Yellow Neck waddling away as fast as his webbed feet could carry him. He laughed and flapped his wings.

Toby gave chase.

"No," bellowed the farmer, who was watching from the farmyard fence.

"Toby, never, ever chase the ducks. Your job is to protect them, not chase them. No!"

Toby didn't mean to chase the duck. It was just that Yellow Neck had nipped him, and it had scared him awake.

The farmer led Toby out of the farmyard and back into his dog paddock. The gate to Toby's dog paddock clanged shut.

Toby slumped into his shed.

Yellow Neck quacked and laughed and pointed. All the other brown ducks joined in.

Toby Dog felt terrible. He had been so excited to meet the new animals on the farm and show off his skills as a livestock guardian dog. But instead of protecting the ducks, he had chased after Yellow Neck. He'd let the farmer down. He'd always prided himself on being a good puppy, and now he had failed. He hung his head in shame.

CHAPTER
❧ 6 ❧

Those earliest days on his farm went by slowly for Toby. He spent most of his time inside his paddock, watching the ducks from the other side of the fence. In the early mornings, the farmer would come to get him and take him to do chores. They would give the birds water and food. The farmer also took time to teach Toby commands such as "come," "sit," and "stay." This was Toby's favorite part of the day because the farmer would give him treats to help him learn new things.

The barn cats would often watch Toby as he did

the chores with the farmer. They usually kept their distance, but Toby could feel their feline eyes watching him constantly.

"Why do you do those tricks for the farmer?" Lil Barn Cat asked Toby one day. "He will give you food regardless of whether you sit or not, dummy."

"I like doing the tricks for the farmer," said Toby. "When I do them, the farmer is happy, and he scratches me behind the ears. That's my favorite part!"

As Toby got closer to the barn cats, Pablo Barn Cat hissed at him and the hair on his back stood up straight.

"Back off," said Lil Barn Cat. "Don't think that we want to be your friends just because we talk to you. We are barn cats. We aren't friends with smelly, slobbery dogs. That's just how we roll."

Toby slumped away from the barn cats. As he trudged back to the duck house, Toby felt sad. While he generally liked his farm, he really wished he had friends. He missed the days of playing with his brothers and sisters on Momma's farm. Here at his farm there was nobody to play with.

"Hey Toby, do you want to play with me?"

Toby lifted his head up to see Samson Puddleduck standing at the edge of the duck yard.

"Sure," said Toby, running over to the large white duck.

Samson quacked happily.

"But there's only one problem," said Toby. "We can't play games like wrestling, hide-and-seek, or tag. The farmer will get mad at me if I chase you. But those are the only games I know."

"Let me teach you a new game," said Samson.

He stuck his duck bill into the snow and drew a three-by-three grid.

"This game is called tic-tac-toe," said Samson. "The way the game works is that one animal draws an X and the other draws an O. The goal is to get three of a kind in a row. When you do that, you win."

"Wow!" exclaimed Toby. "That sounds like a brilliant game. How did you ever come up with something like that?"

"I didn't," said Samson regretfully. "My dad was
the one who taught me how to play."

Toby recalled that Samson's father, Samuel, was
the duck killed by the monster. Toby wondered what
kind of monster would eat a duck.

"I'm really sorry that your dad died," said Toby.
He wasn't sure what to say in this situation, but he
felt like he needed to say something.

"At night, I think the monster is still lurking outside," said Samson. "Sometimes, it will even look into

the window of the duck house when we're sleeping. My mother says it's just a nightmare, but I know that the monster is out there lurking with an evil look on its big furry face."

Toby and Samson spent the rest of that morning playing tic-tac-toe. Sometimes Samson won. Sometimes Toby won. But most of the time, they tied. Eventually, the entire ground was covered in old tic-tac-toe games.

"You kids must clean up that mess soon," said Jemima Puddleduck. "If the farmer were to see that scribbling, you'd have a lot of explaining to do."

Toby swept his tail across the snowy ground, and it erased all the game boards.

"Do you want to play again tomorrow?" asked Toby as he continued to sweep.

"Sure," said Samson. "I like playing games with friends."

And as Toby walked to his paddock, he glowed over that word: *friends*. Samson was Toby's first friend.

CHAPTER
7

Although Toby played games with Samson Puddleduck during the day, he had to stay on his toes as a guard dog at night. Each evening, Toby would hear the frantic yips and howls of the coyotes. Usually, they were very far away. But on the nights they got close, Toby stayed awake all night, barking back at the coyotes. One of the things his mother had taught him was that the coyotes won't get too close if they know that there's a big, barking dog nearby.

Sometimes Toby wondered if Momma had ever seen a monster like the one that killed Samson's father.

She was right about the coyotes. As long as he barked, they didn't get too close. But what about the monster? Was he going to be able to keep it away just by barking?

"Have you ever seen a monster around the farm?" Toby asked the barn cats one night.

Lil Barn Cat, perched upon her usual fence post, glared at him. "There are no monsters. No such thing."

"But Samson Puddleduck says his father was killed by a monster. He saw it with his own duck eyes. And ducks have magnificent eyesight."

Pablo Barn Cat, who was sitting on the next fence post over, shook his head.

"There are lots of things that could kill a duck: coyotes, foxes, weasels, raccoons, hawks, owls. They are all vicious, and they could get a duck right quick. A black bear is bigger than even you, and you're a big, clumsy oaf of a dog. If I were a duck, I'd think a black bear was a monster."

"I asked Samson if it was any of those animals. He said no. He insisted it was a monster," said Toby.

"That's just silliness," said Pablo Barn Cat as he strutted away.

Lil Barn Cat trotted after him.

Later that evening, as Toby walked the barnyard, doing his usual patrol, he was thinking about monsters when a horrid smell hit him.

His nostrils flared as the disgusting smell wafted over him. His sensitive nose burned with the stink. Toby barked to express his anger and confusion.

"Heavens to Betsy! It's a monster!" said a gravelly voice. "I don't mean you no harm, Mr. Monster. I am just a simple skunk passing through these parts."

"Monster? Where's the monster? Who said that? Show yourself," called Toby.

Had the owner of the voice spotted Samson's monster? The air smelled horrible. Maybe the stink was coming from a monster? Although he was frightened, Toby knew that it was his job to protect the farm, even if it meant facing off against a monster.

Toby searched the edge of the fence near the woods, looking, listening, and sniffing near the edge of the pasture. Occasionally he gave a bark of warning.

But no monster, nor any other animal, showed itself.

"Hey, partner? What are you barking at? It doesn't seem safe in these here parts," the gravelly voice sounded behind him again.

Toby whipped around to look for the owner of the voice. There sat a smallish black animal with a white stripe running from the top of his head all the way down to his bushy tail. A skunk!

"Skunk? I don't think I've ever met a skunk before," said Toby. "But I do remember my mother telling me to never pick a fight with one or I'd find myself sleeping in a bathtub full of tomato juice. Whatever that meant."

"Well, let me warn you, Mr. Monster, I am not to be trifled with," said the skunk as he raised his tail and turned his back to Toby. "While I may look small and fragile, I possess some seriously great powers. Just last week, I encountered a gigantic cat that was five times the size of you. She tried to eat me whole, but I gave her a stinking she will never forget."

"A stinking?" inquired Toby.

"Yessiree," said the skunk. "Contained within my body is a set of scent glands that propel forward a powerful spray that stings and stinks anything it touches."

"Well, I can make stinky poops," said Toby. And it was true. When Toby made his doggie poops, they were often quite smelly.

"Ha! Brother, my spray is one thousand times stinkier than any poop you've ever made. Trust me on that one. Even if you were a stallion, your poop wouldn't compare."

Toby contemplated this bizarre statement. This skunk must have a seriously smelly smell. And given how sensitive his nose was, Toby dreaded the thought of smelling such a smell. This skunk creature already smelled horrible. He didn't want to find out how he could smell any worse.

"OK, well, I don't want to fight you," said Toby. "I would just kindly ask that you avoid my ducks and me. My job is to protect the ducks around here."

"That's a fair enough request, Mr. Monster," said the skunk. "While I am partial to the eggs of your ducks, I am an opportunistic omnivore, and I happily eat diggity-ding near everything. So let's make ourselves a deal. I won't spray you or bother any of your ducks if you let me wander the farm at night looking for bugs, grubs, and other yummy things."

Toby didn't like bugs or grubs, so this seemed like a pretty good deal.

"OK," said Toby. "You have a deal."

"Put 'er there, partner," said the skunk as he lowered his tail and offered Toby his front paw. "They call me Grody Otis. What's your name, Mr. Monster?"

"I'm Toby Dog," said Toby as he shook Otis's paw.

And from that night forward, Otis would visit Toby on most evenings.

Each afternoon, as the sun set and the farm grew quiet, the skunk would slip through the fence and make his way over to where Toby was curled up in his doghouse. They would spend hours talking, sharing stories, and swapping jokes as the stars twinkled above them.

One such night, Toby Dog and Grody Otis sat at the edge of the pasture underneath an old oak tree. Toby was sharing a deer bone snack with his skunk pal when a large, shadowy figure swooped down from the sky and landed on a tree branch.

"Good evening, gentlemen," said the creature. "May I join you for a chat?"

Toby was too sur-prised to speak. Grody Otis cocked his head and smiled.

"Victoria! Good to see you," said Otis. "Let me introduce you to Toby Dog. Toby Dog, this is Victoria the Owl. She is one of the smartest creatures you're going to find in these entire woods."

"Uh, nice to meet you," said Toby, feeling a bit nervous. He had never spoken to an owl before, but he did recall seeing her catch a mouse on his first night at the farm. She was quite the talented huntress! And he wasn't sure how he should talk to a huntress. What was the protocol to ensure that she wouldn't try to hunt his ducks?

"So what brings you here, Victoria?" he asked suspiciously.

"I couldn't help but notice you two enjoying the evening," replied Victoria. "I thought I'd come over and say hello."

"Well, we're just enjoying a little snack," said Grody Otis, his nose buried in the end of the deer bone.

"I can see that," said Victoria, eyeing the food. "May I have a taste?" She flew down from the tree.

"Of course," said Toby, nudging the bone closer

to Victoria. He was happy to share his bones. Just not his ducks.

As Victoria nibbled on the bone, she asked Toby questions about himself.

He told her about his duties on the farm, and she listened intently, occasionally interjecting with a word of encouragement or a pointed question.

"You two make an interesting pair," remarked Victoria. "A dog and a skunk, hanging out like the best of friends."

"We sure are," said Grody Otis, smiling at Toby.

"It's true," added Toby. "Grody Otis is my friend."

Victoria nodded in approval. "It's always good to have a friend you can rely on," she said. "Especially on a farm like this. You never know what kind of trouble might come your way."

As Victoria finished picking at the last bits of meat on the bone, she spread her wings.

"It was nice to meet you, Toby Dog. I'm sure we'll run into each other again."

With that, Victoria fluttered her broad wings and

took off into the night sky, leaving Toby and Grody Otis alone under the oak tree.

Well, they weren't really alone. There were always animals scurrying about in the darkness of the surrounding forest. And maybe there was even a monster. Maybe a monster with gigantic claws lurking in the shadows not twenty feet away, jealously eying the deer bone that Toby Dog and Grody Otis continued to enjoy.

CHAPTER
🐾 8 🐾

The weeks passed and Toby grew. Since arriving at the farm a few months earlier, Toby had more than doubled in size. His shaggy white coat had also grown longer to help insulate him during the cold Vermont winters.

His voice grew, too. In his earliest days on the farm, Toby's bark didn't sound very big. But as time went by, his bark got louder and louder. And his voice got deeper and deeper.

Toby was growing up to be a big, strong livestock guardian dog, just like his mother.

And like his mother, Toby often sat on a favorite boulder, watching the farm.

One day he sat on his boulder, looking out on a cold white world. The sun was nowhere to be seen as heavy, wet snow fell from the steely sky. It had been snowing steadily all morning, but because of his thick fur, the snow didn't bother Toby Dog.

It had blanketed the farm over the course of the night, and there was roughly nine inches of powder on the ground by morning.

Toby was contemplating taking a nap after a long night of guard dog duty when he heard someone crying in the distance. It was a curious sound because it wasn't normal crying—it was duck crying. He heard quiet quacks in between the deep, heavy sobs. The sound concerned Toby Dog, so he left his perch to investigate.

Most of the ducks were preening themselves by their pool. It was a ritual that the ducks performed each morning after their first swim of the day.

"Yellow Neck, are there any ducks missing? I heard crying," said Toby.

"Yeah, the Widow Puddleduck scurried off this morning to do her usual," said Yellow Neck. "You can probably find her down in the back corner of the pasture near the tall pine trees."

Toby galloped over to the pine trees and found a big, sobbing pile of feathers. It was Jemima Puddleduck, and she was obviously upset.

"Hey there, Jemima. What's wrong?" asked Toby.

"Oh nothing, dear," responded Jemima. "I just got a little bit of dirt in my eyes. I should probably go wash it out. Nothing for you to be concerned with."

Toby knew that this was a lie. She was crying, but she was probably too embarrassed to explain why.

"It's OK, Jemima," said Toby. "Sometimes I get sad, too, when I think about my mom, my brothers and sisters, and the farm I grew up on. I sometimes miss it so much, and that makes me cry."

A subtle smile flashed across Jemima's duck bill.

"Oh, dear, I know what you mean. Lost loved ones are the most difficult thing. I still think of my darling husband, Samuel Puddleduck, and how he left this earth far too soon."

"Yeah, that's what Samson tells me all the time. He really misses his father."

"Well, my poor Samson was there when it happened. He saw the monster snatch my darling Samuel away. It was quite awful."

"That's what I've heard," said Toby. "Do you know any of the details of what happened to him? Samson says a monster ate him."

"It certainly was a monster," said Jemima. "A big fierce monster with long fur and gigantic sharp paws. He could jump many feet in the air, and he screamed with a devilish scream. It is a scary creature, to be sure."

"But are you sure it was an actual monster?" asked Toby. "Could it have been a coyote or a fox or something like that?"

"There have been many coyotes around here for many years, young puppy. I KNOW the difference," declared Jemima indignantly. "It was clearly not a coyote. Or a fox or a mink or a weasel. It wasn't even

one of those off-looking fisher cats that sometimes come around here. It was a monster that killed my Samuel. A chupacabra or a glawackus! No question about it."

A shudder came over Toby. He didn't even know what a chupacabra or glawackus was, but Jemima did seem quite confident that the creature that killed Samuel was a monster. That thought terrified Toby. Would he have to face a monster one day? And if this monster came back, how would he protect his farm? Toby had become adept at scaring off raccoons, weasels, and the occasional fox. He could also keep the coyotes at bay. But he had yet to face something like a monster.

"Can you tell me about the day it happened?" asked Toby.

"I just did tell you," said Jemima.

"No, I mean, can you give me the details? Tell me the story."

"It's painful, but, yes, I'll tell you," said Jemima. "It was an early morning, and we had just been let out of the duck house for the day. The farmer had poured our water. And Samuel had feasted on his morning grains. He decided to take a nap under a tree—that tree, right there." Jemima gestured toward the tree where the attack took place.

It was very close to the fence, and the fence, at that part of the yard, was very close to the woods.

"An hour later, I was bringing Samson back from his swimming lesson—I was going to leave him with my husband so that I could enjoy a leisurely and quiet breakfast. But before we got to him, a monster leapt over the fence and got into the farmyard."

"Over the fence?" inquired Toby.

"Yes, over the fence," said Jemima.

Toby looked at the fence. That was a pretty serious jump. Nearly five and a half feet! And at the top was an electrical wire that would shock anything that touched it. What kind of animal could jump that high? Even the barn cats, with their excellent jumping ability, couldn't leap over a fence that high.

"The monster rushed at us," said Jemima. "Being

the brave duck that he was, Samuel told Samson and me to run. We flapped our wings as fast as we possibly could, but before we could even turn to run, the monster snatched my beloved Samuel in its mouth. Then it turned and leapt back over the fence and ran off into the woods. That was the last time I ever saw my beloved Samuel."

Toby scratched his ear and thought about what sort of animal could jump that high, attack Samuel, and then jump the fence again, with a fat duck in its mouth.

It would be very hard to jump that high without a duck in your mouth. But to do so with a gigantic duck in your mouth? That seemed impossible. Samuel, if he was anything close to the same size as Samson, would have weighed at least twelve pounds. Maybe Samson and Jemima were right. Maybe this was the work of some sort of magical monster. An *evil* magical monster.

"Well, I'm sorry that your husband passed away," said Toby. "Sounds like he was a very good duck, and it's too bad that he had to go too soon."

"Thank you, Toby," said Jemima. "Now, if you'll excuse me, I am going to get something to eat. I am completely famished after that cry."

Jemima waddled off to the duck feeders while Toby Dog continued examining the fence in disbelief.

As he stood there, he couldn't shake the feeling that he was being watched. He looked around, but he couldn't see anything in the dark woods. Still, the feeling persisted. He sniffed the air, but picked up no monster scent. Cocking his head, he listened intently, trying to hear anything out of the ordinary.

There came a soft rustling in the bushes behind him. He spun around, ready to defend his territory. But he saw nothing. The rustling came again. Toby barked, trying to scare away whatever was slinking around in the shadows. But the rustling continued. Something was out there, and it wasn't going away.

Toby took a few steps toward the bushes, his heart pounding in his chest. He sniffed a big sniff to see if he could identify the creature, but all he could smell was the faint scent of barn cat.

The rustling in the leaves stopped. Toby stood like a statue and stared at the woods for a long time. Watching. Waiting.

CHAPTER
❖ 9 ❖

The next night, Toby watched the farm while the barn cats scratched around the duck feed, searching for rodents. It was a frigid evening, and for Northern Vermont in late January, that's saying something.

"Hey Toby, knock, knock," said Lil Barn Cat.

"Who's there?" asked Toby Dog.

"Scold."

"Scold who?"

"Scold outside."

Pablo and Lil snickered, while Toby looked somewhat confused. The barn cats' jokes never seemed to make much sense to Toby Dog.

Toby was still trying to figure the joke out when his keen sense of hearing picked up a little disturbance in the duck house. As he listened, what had started as a trickle of quacking turned into an avalanche. The ducks set up a wild ruckus, fussing and flapping and quacking.

Toby gave a loud, booming bark and sprinted toward the duck house. He peered through the window. The ducks were clearly agitated, but Toby couldn't identify the source of the disturbance. He gave three quick sniffs to the air.

"If my nose is not deceiving me, there is a raccoon on the farm," said Toby.

Toby circled the duck house, but he couldn't see any raccoons under the house, hiding behind the stilts. He did a second lap around the house, looking at the roof. Nothing. The ducks were still quacking loud and fast. One voice rose above the rest.

"Oh my, oh my. Is it the monster? Samson? Where are you, son?" quavered Jemima Puddleduck.

Toby started a third time around, and that's when he saw him: a big, fat raccoon, hanging on the north corner of the duck house. His front half was inside the building, and his fat backside was hanging out of the building with his legs bouncing up and down as if they were walking on air. It appeared the raccoon had wedged itself into the space between the roof and the wall where the farmer had put chicken wire to allow for ventilation.

That ventilation was a good thing. It ensured that the ducks had access to fresh air. But now, this roly-poly raccoon was trying to fight his way in through the chicken wire that covered the opening.

Toby barked several times. But the raccoon did not turn around. He kept wiggling his hind parts as he tried to force his way into the duck house.

Toby barked again and again. And he tried to leap up and give that chubby rear end a nip, but it was too high for him to reach.

"Pablo! Lil! I need your help," barked Toby.

The barn cats came over to see what was going

on. Pablo and Lil gave one look at the raccoon with his round rump hanging there like a piñata, and Toby jumping and barking and biting at air, and they broke out laughing. The panicked ducks, meanwhile, were all shoving against the little door, trying to get out and onto the ramp so they could waddle to freedom. They were quacking and flapping in such a frenzy, and it seemed as if the building might collapse.

Toby stopped barking to give the barn cats a dirty look.

"You're not helping," he said to the chuckling barn cats.

Then Grody Otis arrived on the scene. "It is a bit funny, partner. You must admit." His nose twitched as he took in the commotion, and there was a grin on his face.

"What in the name of Merry St. Nicholas are you doing?" asked the skunk. "You. Mr. Raccoon. I ask again. Why are you stuck in the duck house like Santa stuck in a chimney?"

"Otis, can you help?" begged Toby.

"What would you like me to do?" replied Grody Otis. "You want me to spray the fat little devil?" He flipped his own little rear end around and lifted his tail.

Toby quickly stopped him. "No! You can't get the raccoon without getting the ducks. And I don't think the farmer would like his ducks smelling like skunk. No offense."

"None taken," said the friendly skunk as he lowered his tail.

Toby said, "Pablo and Lil, do you think you could maybe scratch the raccoon to get him out of there?"

"No way Jose," Lil Barn Cat said firmly. "Our job is to catch rodents, not raccoons."

"Well, raccoons are kind of like big rodents," said Grody Otis.

"Rodent is a scientific classification for mammals in the Rodentia order," stated Pablo Barn Cat with haughty authority. "Raccoons are of the carnivora order, much like us cats, skunks, and dogs. So, as they say, this is not our circus, nor our monkey. You're on your own with this one, Dog."

"Maybe you could try reasoning with him," said Lil Barn Cat sarcastically. "Since your mouth is obviously no good at barking and biting, maybe you can use it to talk him down." Toby thought about this for a moment. Maybe Lil had a good idea.

Since the raccoon was halfway inside the duck house, Toby was forced to speak to the raccoon's hind parts. This felt rather silly, but Toby went ahead with it, nonetheless.

"Excuse me, Raccoon," said Toby loudly so as to be heard over the racket of quacking that had not abated one bit. "Do you have a moment to come out here and speak with me? It's of great importance."

"No, Mojo. No," said the raccoon in a raspy little voice. "Mojo trying to get eggs. Mojo needs eggs. Egg raid by Mojo."

"Well, I'm the guard dog at this here farm, and I would really like you to not take our duck eggs. I also don't want you to harm our ducks."

"Mojo no harm no ducks," declared the raccoon. "Egg raid only."

Toby turned to the Barn Cats and Grody Otis. "Did he say his name is Mojo?"

"I can't hear a thing with all the infernal quacking going on," said Grody Otis. "And don't ask me to try to figure out raccoons. They are weird creatures."

"Yeah. They eat trash," said Lil, absolutely disgusted. "Like they take honest-to-goodness garbage from inside the can, put it in their mouth, and then eat it. And they like it, too!"

Toby Dog had always been curious about raccoons. He remembered the first time he'd seen one, back when he was just a pup at Momma's farm. He'd been playing in the river with his brothers and sisters when he spotted a group of raccoons washing their little paws downstream. He had been fascinated by the way they moved, so agile and graceful despite their bulk. He had wanted to go over and say hello, but his mother cautioned him against it, warning that raccoons could be unpredictable.

Besides that one early encounter, Toby had not had any other opportunities to observe raccoons up close. They were not common on the farm where he lived, and he had always been too busy with his duties as a livestock guardian dog to go looking for them. But he thought they were intelligent and resourceful creatures, so when he saw this fat raccoon stuck in the duck house, he was rather disappointed. This raccoon seemed to be one big disaster.

"Well, Mr. Mojo, sir, I need to ask you to get out of the duck house," said Toby. "I'm sorry, but I must insist."

"After egg raid, Mojo leave."

"If you don't come out, I'm gonna have to wake up the farmer. And he's probably gonna come out here with his boom stick. And I don't think you'll like what happens after that."

"No, no boom stick," said the raccoon. "Mojo don't like no boom sticks. Mojo don't like people either."

"Well, Mr. Mojo, I suggest you end your little egg raid and get out of here," said Toby.

"Mojo coming down." The raccoon began to struggle and squirm, but he seemed to be stuck. He planted his back legs on the wall and pushed, but his front half remained in the duck house. Eventually, his body went limp.

"Mojo stuck," said the raccoon in a resigned tone.

"I do believe we have a problem on our hands," said Toby to the barn cats and Grody Otis. "I don't want to call the farmer because he'll probably kill this raccoon. But how can I help get him out?"

"That seems like way more effort than it's worth," said Lil Barn Cat.

"Any ideas, Grody Otis?" asked Toby.

The skunk scratched his chin with his paw and thought for a moment.

"What if we tried to pull him out?" said Grody Otis.

"That's an idea," said Toby. "We could tie a rope around his legs and give him a good, hard yank. But where can I get a rope?"

"This has disaster written all over it," said Lil Barn Cat.

"I know," exclaimed Toby, and he ran off toward the water hydrant. When he returned, he had the farmer's water hose in his mouth. "Grody Otis, do you think you can climb up there and tie this end of the hose around Mojo?"

The skunk grabbed the hose from Toby and scampered up the side of the duck house. He wrapped the hose around the raccoon several times.

"That sure tickles the Mojo." The raccoon giggled.

The skunk eyed the raccoon with a mischievous glint in his eye. He had always been fascinated by knots, and he decided today was a good day to try his hand at a new knot he was learning. So Grody Otis set to work, fumbling and pulling, working to create a secure knot.

"Hey, what's your mojo doing over there?" exclaimed Mojo. "Mojo don't like it one bit."

"Hang tight, Mr. Mojo," said Toby. "We're gonna get you out of there."

The raccoon, understandably, was not amused by this turn of events and was writhing and scratching at the hose, trying to escape. The skunk, however, was determined to succeed, and he continued to tug and wrap the hose around the raccoon. It was a comical sight, with the skunk's tongue sticking out in concentration and the raccoon's fur standing on end in alarm.

Toby took the hose in his mouth and dragged it away from the duck house, pulling harder and harder on the raccoon.

"Mojo, mojo, mojo!" yelped the raccoon.

With one last mighty tug, the raccoon came flying out of the duck house and fell to the ground.

He seemed dazed.

The quacking died down considerably. There were still some offended mutterings.

And Jemima was smothering Samson, apparently because he said, "Ma, I can't breathe."

"I don't know what I'd do if the monster took you, too," Jemima answered.

"It wasn't the monster, Ma. Don't worry. I'm not going anywhere."

Grody Otis scrambled down and untied his knot. "Super," he said. "Did you see that, partner?" he asked Toby Dog. "That knot was a thing of beauty."

The raccoon blinked several times, trying to focus. When his vision finally cleared, he saw that he was surrounded by the barn cats, Grody Otis, and Toby.

"Mojo is outta here!" he said as he rolled over onto his feet.

"Please don't come back," Toby Dog politely shouted as the fat raccoon scampered (as fast as a fat raccoon can scamper) through a hole in the fence and into the woods.

"Well, I guess the good news is you got the raccoon out," said Pablo Barn Cat. "But the bad news is the farmer is not going to like what you did to his hose."

Toby looked down at the hose. Dismay flashed across his face. His teeth had punctured the hose. In several places.

That next morning, when the farmer came outside to let the ducks out, he noticed the hose had been strewn all about the ground and chewed upon.

"Toby!" bellowed the farmer. "What did you do?"

Toby sheepishly approached the farmer with his tail between his legs. He attempted to lick the farmer's hand, but the farmer was in no mood for that.

"You ruined my best hose," scolded the farmer. "No chewing hoses!"

Toby whimpered a protest. He tried to gesture

toward the hole that Mojo had created in the side of the duck house.

It took the farmer a moment, but he eventually noticed where Toby was looking. "What are you looking at, boy? What's up there?"

He stepped up to the corner of the duck house and saw that an opening had been ripped through the ventilation screen. He also noticed a good deal of raccoon fur caught in the wire.

"Did something go on last night that I'm not aware of?" asked the farmer.

Toby gave a bark and wagged his tail.

The farmer counted the ducks. "All present and accounted for," he said. "Good boy, Toby Dog." He scratched Toby behind the ears.

He never did figure out how a raccoon had gotten through the fence and up into the duck house. (Toby, Pablo, and Lil never spilled the beans.) And he was still miffed that Toby chewed up his hose. But the ducks were safe in the end. And that was the most important thing.

The farmer gave Toby a nice deer hoof to chew on. "That is what you chew. Not my hoses. Got it?"

Toby wagged his tail.

CHAPTER
🐾 10 🐾

One beautiful crisp February morning, Toby Dog had done a particularly good job with his farm chores, and the farmer rewarded him with a huge bowl of kibble and beef, with a delicious duck egg on top. The bowl looked absolutely scrumptious with the yolk shining like a sunrise. Toby sat patiently, drooling from the corners of his mouth as he waited for the farmer to give him the signal to start chowing down. "Enjoy, buddy boy," said the farmer cheerfully before walking away.

But as soon as the farmer was out of sight, Pablo

Barn Cat and Lil Barn Cat crept in, forming a Toby Dog sandwich. "OK, buddy, you know what to do now?" said Pablo, with a sly look. "Take three steps back and let us get our chomps first."

Lil Barn Cat was eyeing the pile of ground beef in the corner of the bowl.

Toby's heart sank. This might be the best meal of his entire life, and he was not going to let the obnoxious and condescending barn cats eat his food. After weeks of always giving them first dibs, Toby was done being polite. A low growl started to emanate from the base of his belly, and both barn cats froze in terror. Toby's lips curled into a snarl that would have sent fear into the bravest of barn cats.

"Take it easy, Toby Dog. We didn't mean anything by it," said Pablo, trying to calm him down.

"Yeah, we're your friends," added Lil Barn Cat, trying to save face. "Remember, you like to share with your friends."

"Friends don't steal friends' breakfast," said Toby firmly.

"We were just tasting it to make sure it was OK for you to eat. It's definitely OK for you to eat. You should eat it. Definitely. We're not going to bother you. Go on ahead," said Pablo, trying to backtrack.

With the departure of the barn cats, Toby relaxed a little bit. Had that really worked? Was he able to scare away the barn cats with just a growl? Toby savored his breakfast, leisurely taking bites and gulps until his belly was full.

But there was still a bit left in the bowl. "Hey, Pablo Barn Cat! Hey, Lil Barn Cat! Are you guys still hungry?" asked Toby, warily. The barn cats emerged from the rafters of the shed, looking cautious and scared.

"I'm always happy to share my breakfast with my friends," said Toby. "Just let me have the first bite, OK?"

Lil Barn Cat tentatively climbed down from the rafters and began to sniff at the bowl, followed by Pablo. "Enjoy, friends," said Toby, feeling proud for standing up for himself.

That moment seemed to be a bit of a turning point for Toby Dog. As the days went by, the farm reached the depths of winter. The nights grew colder, and the snow became deeper.

Toby Dog had been living on the farm for a few months now, and it was finally starting to feel like home. And now, even the barn cats had become friends. No more hissing and spitting from them.

After he shared his meal with them that day, they started hanging out with him in the evenings, lounging in his dog shed and chatting about the day's events.

Toby was delighted by this shift. He'd always been a social dog, and Grody Otis and Samson were fine friends. But there was always room for more friends. The barn cats were still surly, to be sure, but they were also smart and funny, and they had interesting stories to tell. Toby listened attentively as they shared their tales of hunting mice and exploring the farm. He enjoyed their company and looked forward to their visits each night.

As Toby's friendship with the barn cats deepened, he began to see them as a kind of extended family, and he was grateful to have them in his life. They helped him feel more connected to the farm and to the animals that lived there. They showed him that home was not just a place, but a feeling, and that it could be found in the most unexpected places.

Toby knew he still had much to learn about life on the farm, but he was no longer a stranger. He was a part of the community now, and he was happy to be here. He looked forward to the adventures that lay ahead, and he knew he'd always have the barn cats by his side. Together, they'd face whatever challenges came their way, and they'd make the most of their time on the farm. One night they were all together, enjoying the moonrise. Toby curled up in the hay. The barn cats perched on a rafter in his shed.

"Yip yip yeooooow!" the coyotes called from the distance.

The hair on Lil Barn Cat's back stood on end. "They are getting too close for comfort. Do you mind doing something about that, Dog?"

Toby got up from chewing his bone and stepped outside. He gave a few loud barks, and the coyotes quieted down. Toby turned to go back inside, but he stopped when his nose detected the unique odor of Grody Otis.

"How's it going tonight, buddy?" asked Grody Otis.

"Not too bad," said Toby. "A little bored, but what can you do?"

"I'll tell you what you can do," exclaimed the skunk. "You can come wander the pasture with me. We can look for this mythical monster that you're always talking about. Let's go!"

"Go?" asked Toby. "I can't go. I'm supposed to stay here in my pen and guard the farm."

"Don't be an old stick in the mud," said Grody Otis. "I know of a spot along the fence line where you can sneak right through."

Toby considered this idea for a moment. Grody Otis was right. There were all sorts of holes in the old farm fence, and with a little effort and a healthy amount of digging, Toby could sneak out.

"OK," said Toby. "I can come out, but only for a while. If I don't make it back here in time for morning chores, the farmer will be awfully mad at me."

"Not a good idea," said Lil.

"No, no," Pablo added. "Cats may wander. Dogs may not."

"I'll get you back in plenty of time, pal!" Grody Otis said. "The farmer will never know."

Toby and Grody Otis walked along the fence until they came to a spot that had a good-sized hole. Using their paws, the two friends made the hole much larger, and Toby squirmed his way through the opening and out of the barnyard.

They scampered together across the pasture.

Although the farmer frequently took him out to the field to run and play, Toby had never been out in the pasture at night. The smells and sounds were a new and different experience. Toby also felt a strange feeling in the pit of his stomach. He knew he was being naughty, and he shouldn't be doing this, but he also knew he was enjoying himself.

Toby and Grody Otis dashed through the pasture for a good long while until they finally reached the farthest side of the pasture near the edge of the dark woods. But they were having so much fun that they hadn't even noticed how far they had gone until they heard a howl.

"Look what we have here," growled a familiar voice.

Toby turned to see a large and mangy coyote standing near a large oak tree. Behind her stood two smaller coyotes.

"It looks like a house dog has found his way onto our turf," said the largest coyote. "What do we do to house dogs on our turf, guys?"

"Oh, I know, I know," said the smallest of the three coyotes. "We give them a serious chomping! Isn't that right, Jessica?"

The other coyotes chuckled. All three began to circle Toby menacingly.

"Excuse me, coyote crew," said Grody Otis. Walking backward, he stepped between Toby and the coyotes. "While I'm sure you would love to use my pal Toby here as a fluffy white chew toy, I would like to call your attention to the small skunk with his hindquarters pointed in your general direction."

Looks of fear briefly flashed over the faces of the coyotes.

"Toby, I'm going to start counting. And when I get to three, I want you to run as far and fast as you possibly can."

"But what about you?" asked Toby.

"Don't worry about me," said the skunk. "Just get yourself away from here."

The coyotes growled and snarled.

"One," said Grody Otis.

The two smaller coyotes began to back away from Toby and Grody Otis, but the larger coyote held her ground.

"Two," continued Grody Otis. There was a certain devilish tone to his voice.

Toby looked to his left and saw an opening to a path at the forest's edge. This would be the direction he would head.

"Three!" exclaimed Grody Otis.

A cloud of yellowish mist shot from Otis's backside. It hit the largest coyote directly in the face. And while this spray was impressive, it was not nearly as attention grabbing as the stench that accompanied it.

"Don't just stand there admiring my masterpiece!" yelled Grody Otis. "Run, Toby, run!"

Heeding Otis's advice, Toby took off for the path at the edge of the woods. He heard the largest coyote whimper as he ran away.

Alone, Toby ran through the dark forest. His heart raced as he jumped over tree stumps and ducked under branches and pricker bushes. The snow on the ground made running difficult and tiring. But Toby kept running for his life.

CHAPTER
🐾 11 🐾

The farmer had taken Toby hiking in the woods from time to time.

Toby always enjoyed going into the woods on those walks. But he had never been in the woods alone, and he had never been in the woods in the dark.

In the middle of the night, in the dead of winter, being alone was terrifying.

After Toby was confident he'd outrun the coyotes, he slowed down to catch his breath. It took several minutes for his heart to slow down.

But finally he stopped sucking in air and his heart

stopped feeling like it would burst from his chest.

He looked around to see where he was. He had no clue. He took a sniff. Recognized no familiar scent. He definitely was pretty far away.

Ordinarily, Toby's sensitive nose would help point him in the direction of his farm, and he'd be able to wander his way back to the pasture. But the woods made things trickier. Because they were filled with trees, it made it hard to pick up the scent of something like a duck. In addition, the woods were filled with so many unfamiliar animal smells from all sorts of creatures that Toby had never met. Those strange smells sent Toby confusing directional signals, making it impossible for him to know which way was home.

He stood still, listening.

Again the trees hindered him. They blocked sounds. They muffled sounds. Or sounds bounced into the woods from one direction and ricocheted off icy, bare trunks and limbs until Toby had no way of knowing where the sound had originated.

Not knowing which way to go, Toby took a deep sniff of the air and made his best guess, walking in the direction he hoped would take him back to his farm.

After walking for a bit, Toby found a stream. Maybe this was a good sign because Toby knew that there was a stream near his farm. And he thought maybe if he just followed the stream, he'd find his home. So he changed direction and followed the stream.

Toby walked farther and farther, but the farther he walked, the more he second-guessed himself, wondering if he was going in the right direction. What if he was going in the complete opposite direction? What if he would never see the farmer again? Or Samson and Jemima Puddleduck? Toby even worried that he might never see the surly barn cats again. And what about Grody Otis? Had he escaped the coyotes?

Not knowing what else to do, Toby kept going. After a good deal more walking, he came to a field. It lay across the road and it was unfenced.

He sniffed. Nothing familiar. But still, this had

to be the right direction, didn't it? There was a wide-open field near his farm. That field belonged to his neighbors. He was excited. This field was so close to his home. So Toby, thinking he was going in the right direction, darted toward the field.

He'd only taken a few steps when an ear-piercing, honking sound broke through the air.

Toby screeched to a stop.

A brilliant flash of bright headlights was bearing down on him.

Toby jumped back just in time. He narrowly avoided being transformed from a farm dog into a farm-dog pizza.

"Watch where you're going, you stupid mutt!" screamed the driver as he sped off.

The farmer had always warned Toby to stay away from the road. Now that warning made sense.

Toby was now terrified. He felt like he was about to cry. But not wanting to stand in the middle of the road crying, Toby crossed over and headed into the open field.

Toby Dog wandered for another hour, his paws crunching through the snow as he searched for his farm. He had no idea how he had gotten so lost, but he was determined to find his way back. He was not one to give up easily. He stopped to sniff the air again. And . . . could it be? He thought he smelled his farm.

As he made his way through the snow-covered landscape, he came upon a pasture that was over-grown and tangled with brush and scrub. It was clear that this pasture had once been a wide-open hayfield, but neglect and unchecked growth had turned it into a wild, untamed place. It was hard to traverse, with brambles snagging at Toby's fur and branches scratch-ing at his face. But he pressed on, following the faint scent of his farm.

He had been wandering for what felt like an eter-nity when he finally saw something that gave him hope. It was a patch of raspberry bushes, their ber-ries silhouetted against the snow, standing out like beacons. Toby's mouth watered at the sight, and he hurried over to investigate.

As Toby drew closer, he saw that something was wrong. The raspberries were withered and black, and there was a strange, sickly smell in the air. Toby sniffed and recoiled in disgust. They were rotten and frozen, and it was clear that no one had picked them in a long time.

Toby couldn't believe his bad luck.

He turned away from the berries, feeling deflated and disappointed.

As he trudged on through the overgrown pasture, his spirits fell lower and lower. He was tired and hungry, and he was starting to worry that he might never find his farm. The scent he'd had of his farm had faded, and he had no idea how he was going to get home. He was just about to give up when he saw something that made his heart skip a beat. Was it the porch light on his farm?

He surged forward.

But it was not the farm. It was just a mirage—the moonlight reflecting off an icy tree branch.

Toby barked in frustration and disappointment,

and he slumped down in the snow. He was lost and alone, and he didn't know if he'd ever see his farm again.

"Oof. Get off me, big guy," an anxious voice said.

Toby felt something wiggle under him.

He lifted his tail and looked beneath it and found he was sitting on an animal.

The animal sprang up and kicked Toby right in the head, and then tripped over Toby's front legs and did a face plant.

Toby fell backward and saw stars for a moment.

Still somewhat dazed, Toby picked up his head and looked to see what had kicked him. There, quivering in front of him, was a white-tailed deer—a teenage buck. He looked as scared as Toby felt.

"Oh, I'm so sorry," apologized the deer. "I didn't mean to kick you. I mean, did I really even kick you? I'm so, so sorry if I did, sir. Did I kick you?"

"It's OK," said Toby.

The deer untangled his front legs and got to his feet, getting ready to scamper off.

Before he could dart away, Toby blurted out, "You wouldn't happen to know if my farm is around here, would you?"

"Oh, well, take your pick. There are a lot of farms around here," said the deer.

"I know," said Toby. "But I'm looking for one particular farm. Well, sorry to bother you. It was nice meeting you."

"Well, it was very nice to meet you, too," said the deer. "Always nice to meet a new friend. Because you know I've been quite lonely lately. My friends seem to be disappearing." He threw a nervous look over his shoulder and lowered his voice. "I've seen lots of people in the woods lately. They're all wearing brightly colored clothing. And they have boom sticks. I haven't gotten too close to them because they make me nervous."

Toby's heart sank a little for the young deer. He knew what was probably happening. The farmer would often go hunting for deer.

The deer continued whispering. "And so many

of my friends have disappeared. Tony and Bobby and Petey? All gone! And the four of us used to wander around the far woods. But now I'm on my own."

Toby squirmed a little. Sometimes, after the farmer went hunting, he would give Toby Dog tasty things to chew on, like deer hooves. Or he'd put delicious deer organ meat into his food dish. A guilty frown flashed across Toby's face.

"I can probably try to help you find your farm," said the deer. "Can I come with you and bed down at your place?"

Toby thought for a moment about bringing a deer back to the farm. He didn't believe that would work well for the farm or the deer. "I wouldn't want to trouble you. I'm sure I can find it soon."

Toby and the young deer headed off in separate directions.

As he walked onward, Toby couldn't shake the feeling of guilt that washed over him as he thought about Tony and Bobby and Petey, who had disappeared from the woods. But deer were not the animals he was supposed to protect. He had his own animals, and he needed to get back to the farm and take up his responsibilities. The farm was currently unprotected, and worse than that, the coyotes knew it was unprotected. They'd seen him scampering off into the woods. Toby walked faster through the overgrown field.

On the other side?

More woods.

CHAPTER
🐾 12 🐾

Toby trotted for a few miles, following a stream, but he had no luck finding his way back to the farm. It was still dark, but the moon had set and the color of the sky was shifting, turning that blackish blue that you always see right before sunrise.

Toby crossed yet another field and found another patch of woods. He was not too far into the new woods when something that looked like a pile of feathers swooped down to the trail in front of him, snatched something from the ground, and fluttered back upward. The incident happened no more than eighteen inches from Toby's face.

Toby was shocked. He cocked his head toward a nearby maple tree. And there, in the branches of the tree, he saw a large barred owl chomping on a freshly caught mouse. It was the same owl that he had seen at the farm months earlier.

"Oh, hello. I'm sorry if I scared you," said the owl. "I was just grabbing my late, late, late-night snack before I turn in for the evening."

Toby was too stunned to speak.

"Like I said, I didn't mean to spook you," said the owl. "Do you remember me? My name is Victoria."

"R-r-r-r-right," stammered Toby.

"Well, nice to see you again, Toby. You're a bit far from the duck farm today, aren't you?"

"Yes, I am," said Toby. "Do you know where it is? Can you point me in the right direction? I'm a little lost right now."

"Not a problem at all, my boy. No problem at all."

Victoria swooped down from the tree and landed on a tree stump.

"You know, I've had my eye on that farm for quite some time," confided Victoria. "Lots of ducks. Ducks are tasty!"

Toby was stunned by this admission from the owl. Toby's job was to protect all the animals on his farm. How could he let this creature come to his farm and eat some of his birds? This made Toby's blood boil.

"You can't do that," growled Toby. "That's my farm. My job is to protect it."

"Well, you seem to be doing a fine job protecting it all the way out here," quipped the owl. "What are you doing wandering over here if you're supposed to be protecting your farm?"

Toby's fluffy white tail drooped between his legs. His sense of embarrassment overtook his anger. One of the most fundamental responsibilities of the guard dog is to guard his animals. And meanwhile, here he was, with no idea how far away from his farm he was, asking a strange owl for directions.

"I was chasing some coyotes away, and I, uh, got a little turned around," said Toby. And then he added, "Well, no, that's not exactly true. I went out to look for a monster. A terrible monster who took one of our ducks. A long time ago. Before I lived on my farm. But I didn't find the monster. I found some coyotes, instead. And Grody Otis was going to spray them, so he told me to run."

"That's understandable," said Victoria in a very gracious tone. "I know you're just doing your job, much like I am just doing my job. Every creature in this world has its own job to do, and you can't get mad at them for doing that job. I think the expression is, 'Don't get mad at the rain for being wet.'"

Victoria's words confused Toby. What rain was she even talking about?

"Now I'm no fan of those coyotes," continued Victoria. "In fact, they're actually competition for me. Did you know a coyote's diet primarily consists of mice and other small rodents?"

"I didn't know that," said Toby. "I thought they just wanted to eat my ducks."

"But have they ever eaten your ducks?" asked Victoria.

"Well, no," said Toby. "Not that I know of, at least."

"So then, how do all these coyotes survive? They've never eaten your ducks. That means they have to be eating something else."

"You've got a point there."

"I like to think of the forest and the farms that surround it as a bit of an ecosystem," explained Victoria. "We all play our part. We all have our job. And we can't fault folks for doing their jobs. I wouldn't fault you if you were to bark at me to keep me away from your ducks. You're just doing your job, protecting the farmer's food. That's how it all works. And while we might not like getting wet when it rains, without the rain, the plants couldn't grow. We need the rain, just like we need the coyotes."

Toby thought about this statement. Victoria's words rang true. All the animals he knew were just trying to survive, and he couldn't blame them for doing the things they needed to do.

"I'm sorry I growled at you earlier," said Toby.

"Quite alright, good sir," said Victoria with a gracious flap of her left wing.

"Earlier you said you knew where my farm was. Do you mind giving me directions?"

"Absolutely not, my boy. You're not that far at all. You're less than half a mile away."

Toby was stunned. He couldn't believe he was that close to his farm. He imagined being miles and miles away. A half mile? If he ran, he could make it back before the farmer woke up.

"I'll tell you what. I'll lead you right there to it. Let's go."

And with a mighty flap of her wings, Victoria took off.

Toby jogged after her.

Victoria was correct. The farm was not far. Just a little way through the forest, and Toby found himself at the back end of the farmer's pasture. Quacking ducks and the scent of barn cats filled Toby Dog's ears and nose.

"Well, my boy, I think you can find your way back home from here," said Victoria as she landed in a nearby birch tree.

Toby wondered if he'd see Victoria again and if she'd ever try to take one of his ducks.

"I'll keep an eye out for you, Toby Dog," said the owl. "I like the cut of your jib. You seem like a good one. And as long as you can let me have some mice, I'll stay away from your ducks and geese."

"You've got yourself a deal," said Toby.

He was about to run down the hill when he suddenly stopped and turned toward Victoria. She seemed to know a lot, and this might be his only chance to ask her. "Victoria, can I ask you a question?" inquired Toby.

"You just asked one," said Victoria. "But go ahead and ask one more."

"You seem to know all the creatures in this area." Toby cleared his throat nervously. "And as you said, you've never eaten ducks from our farm, and the coyotes have never eaten ducks from our farm. But some creature ate my friend's father. Samuel Puddleduck was the poor fellow's name. All the animals say it was a monster that took him. Have you ever seen a monster? How can I protect my farm against monsters? Do you have any advice?"

"There are no such things as monsters, my dear boy." Victoria chuckled. "There are just other animals like you and me. I don't know what ate your friend's father. But I can tell you this: Whatever it was, it was just another animal. And unless it was a black bear, just about any other animal of the forest would be scared off by a big, strapping pup like yourself. Just have some confidence and stand your ground. You should be OK. Heck, I'm sure that there are a lot of animals out there that would consider *you* to be the monster, my friend."

Toby chuckled at Victoria's words. The barred owl leapt from her perch and took off into the sky. Toby watched her fly away into the orange and purple dawn sky. Looking toward his barn, Toby noticed that the sun was just creeping up beyond the horizon. If he acted quickly, he'd be able to sneak back into the barnyard.

CHAPTER
🐾 13 🐾

Toby Dog sprinted down the hill toward the barn, his legs pumping and his tongue lolling out of his mouth. He was bone-tired from his long trek and ready for a nap as soon as he finished his morning chores.

He was just sliding through the hole in the fence when he heard a shrieking noise that stopped him dead in his tracks. It was a loud, high-pitched wail that tore through the peaceful dawn and sent shivers down Toby's spine.

His heart began to pound a million miles per

hour. What could have made that horrific noise?

He sniffed the air, trying to get a sense of what was going on. And what he could distinctly smell was Pablo Barn Cat and Lil Barn Cat. But there was the scent of a third cat, too—an unfamiliar one.

Toby's hackles rose as he cautiously approached the barn. He wasn't sure what he was going to find, but he knew it couldn't be good. He peeked his head around the door and scanned the dim interior.

As he rounded the corner and moved up the high drive of the barn—the ramp leading to the second floor—he saw Lil Barn Cat and another creature that looked like a large, odd-looking cat. The beast was chasing Lil, who quickly scurried up one of the barn posts and into the rafters.

The attacking animal turned toward Pablo Barn Cat and growled.

Pablo Barn Cat had puffed up his fur to look nearly twice his regular size. But as big as Pablo Barn Cat was, he was nowhere near the size of the fierce cat creature he was facing.

The creature looked like a cat, but she was missing her tail. Tufts of hair grew outward from her face, and she had big fluffy feet and gigantic paws. Toby could only assume that the claws attached to those paws were large and sharp.

Toby's instincts kicked in and he rushed toward the intruder, barking and snapping. He had to protect his mates, even if the barn cats were surly and ungrateful.

The creature snarled and swiped at Toby, her claws narrowly missing his face. Toby backed off, barking again to distract the creature. He had to keep her focused on him, away from the vulnerable barn cats.

But the creature was fast and agile, and she kept coming at Toby with relentless ferocity. Toby knew he couldn't keep away from her sharp claws for long.

As he dodged away from the cat for the twentieth time, Toby suddenly had a realization. He knew right then and there that *this* was the monster. Whatever this creature was, she fit the description that he had heard over and over again from Samson and Jemima Puddleduck. But thinking back to Victoria's words, he also realized this wasn't really a monster. This was just another animal of the forest. And she was a good deal smaller than Toby.

Regardless of what this creature was, she was on his farm and attacking animals on his farm. Toby needed to act quickly. A fierce growl originated from Toby's belly and burst out of his mouth. His lips curled and large white teeth were fully displayed.

Lil Barn Cat's head snapped around to see the source of the growl. A look of surprise registered on her face. That was definitely Toby Dog, but it didn't sound anything like the good-natured fluff ball who was often the butt of her jokes. It was like a switch had been flipped, and just like that, the goofy puppy was gone. He'd transformed into a monster.

The creature heard the horrible, menacing growl as well. She whipped her head around and looked toward Toby.

"Get out of here, dog!" shrieked the creature.

"This ain't your fight."

"This is my farm and the barn cats are my friends," growled Toby. "You need to leave right now."

Still snarling, Toby advanced on the creature.

The creature faced Toby.

Pablo Barn Cat saw his chance to escape, and he sprinted up a barn post to join Lil Barn Cat in the rafters.

The creature crouched and moved slowly toward Toby.

While she seemed quite fearsome and her claws were indeed sharp, Toby realized that the creature was only half his size. Maybe he could intimidate the wild animal and avoid a fight.

The creature sprang, launching herself through the air, quick as lightning. Both front claws were aimed right at Toby's face.

Toby dodged.

The wild animal swung back around and slashed at Toby's hindquarter, raking her razor-sharp claws through his fur.

He yelped in pain.

Blood dripped from his behind, and he knew that he was in trouble.

The creature circled him, no doubt preparing for another attack. It was an unsettling sight, with her tufted fur standing on end and eyes glowing like fiery coals. Toby bared his teeth and growled.

But the creature was not impressed. She pulled back and swatted at Toby again, her claws just missing his face.

Toby felt the wind on his nose, and he knew he had to do something fast. He couldn't keep dodging and evading forever.

"I don't want to hurt you," growled Toby, "but you'll be very sorry if you don't leave right now."

The creature seemed to hesitate for a moment, as if considering Toby's words. Then she let out a low, guttural growl and sprang forward.

Toby dodged to the side. But the creature was quick and nimble, and turned on a dime, and this time she landed on Toby at full force, with her mighty arms wrapped around Toby's neck.

Toby yelped and snarled and scratched and bit.

The two animals rolled around the barn floor, a tornado of flashing claws, gnashing teeth, and wild intensity.

They rolled into a barn post and split apart, two raging balls of fury.

"You're the one who is going to be sorry," snarled the animal as she circled him.

Toby's fur was matted red with blood.

The creature was relentless, attacking with ferocity and speed.

She swatted.

Toby dodged.

She swatted again.

Toby dodged again.

She swatted a third time.

But this time, Toby caught the creature's foreleg in his mouth and clamped down hard, refusing to let go.

The creature shrieked in agony, thrashing and

struggling to escape. She raked the claws of her free paw down Toby's back.

But Toby held on. He stood up tall, lifting the creature off the ground. Then he whipped his head back and forth several times, shaking the creature violently. Finally, he released the leg and stepped back, panting.

The animal tried to limp away into the cold, snowy dawn. Even with a broken leg, the creature was fast. Running on three legs, she darted for the fence.

Toby barked his big, booming bark and gave chase.

The creature squeezed through the fence and, quick as lightning, she disappeared into the dark woods. Toby raced through the snow, his paws pounding the ground, as he chased after the creature. He could hear the wild thing breathing hard and also the sound of heavy footsteps racing through the underbrush. The wild animal wasn't trying to be stealthy—she was going on adrenaline, blindly trying to escape.

Toby's adrenaline was pumping just as hard. He ran blindly—his heart pounding in his chest and his breath coming in short, ragged gasps. He refused to give up. He had to catch the creature and make sure that she never came back.

As the sound of the creature tromping through the woods faded away, Toby stopped to listen. Had she gotten away? No. He could hear her panting. She had just stopped running.

And there she was. Up ahead, bloody fur glinted crimson in the slowly rising sun. The wild animal was lying in the snow, looking terrified and exhausted.

He circled the creature to gauge how much fight and fury she had left.

She looked back at Toby Dog with a gaze full of fear, but her teeth were bared in a snarl.

Toby pounced, tackling the cat to the ground and pinning her beneath his weight.

She dug her claws into his fur, but the animal did not have enough strength to get through his fur and down to his skin. She gave a pitiful cry and went limp. The battle was clearly over.

Toby Dog drew away from the wild cat.

He sat in the snow, panting. He had just won a fierce battle against a vicious wild animal, and he was feeling proud of himself. He had defended his farm and his home, and he had proven that he was a capable and courageous dog.

But as he sat there, he couldn't help but wonder about what Victoria had said earlier. "Don't get mad at the rain for being wet." What had she meant by that? Toby thought about it for a moment, trying to puzzle out the meaning of Victoria's words. He knew that the wild cat had been a threat to his farm, but she was no longer a threat. He had defeated her, and she was unlikely to come back.

So should he show mercy? Should he let her go, or should he finish the job to make sure that she would never again threaten his farm? It was a difficult decision, and Toby wasn't sure what to do.

Slowly, Toby stepped back and looked carefully at this creature. This creature wasn't just a creature. She was a bobcat. Toby was pretty sure that was the name for the wild, nearly tailless cats that wandered these woods.

The bobcat stood on three feet, turned, and limped away. Toby continued to bark until the creature disappeared behind the large pine trees. As the scent of the animal abated, Toby stopped his barking. He knew that he had done the right thing. He was doing his job; the bobcat was just doing the same.

For several minutes more, Toby stood at the edge of the woods barking loudly, declaring that this farm was his farm and no animals were allowed to mess with his farm. It felt good to make that declaration through his barking.

Feeling exhausted, Toby eventually turned around and walked back toward the farm. He looked at his wounds. They didn't hurt much, but they continued to drip blood.

When Toby got back to his yard, the farmer was waiting for him.

"I don't believe it, buddy," said the farmer. "Did you just take on a bobcat?"

Toby licked the farmer's outstretched hand.

The farmer bent down to examine Toby's wounds. "Oh man, we're gonna have to do something about these."

The farmer raced through the morning chores—gave the birds their food and water—and then loaded Toby Dog into the pickup truck.

Toby wondered where they were going, but he

was too exhausted to stay awake and watch out the window. He slept soundly in the passenger seat of the truck as it rumbled down the road.

CHAPTER
🐾 14 🐾

The gray pickup truck rolled back into the farm's driveway like a thundercloud, its tires spitting gravel as it came to a halt. The farmer climbed out from behind the wheel, his worn rubber boots splashing in the muddy driveway. He walked around to the passenger side, opened the door, and reached in to lift Toby out of the cab and gently place him on the ground.

Toby's legs felt wobbly as he hit the ground. His hindquarters were still sore from the battle with the bobcat. He'd been lucky to come out of the fight with just a few scratches and one bite, but he had still needed to go to the vet to get stitched up. The trip hadn't been terrible, but the cone they'd wrapped around his neck to keep him from licking his wounds made him feel like a fool.

The cone was a monstrosity—a white plastic bulb attached to an orange collar that shone like a beacon in the early-morning light. Toby felt self-conscious as he limped toward the barn, aware of the other animals snickering. But he didn't let it get to him. He was just happy to be home and in one piece.

The farmer loomed over him, a broad smile on his weathered face. "You did good, boy," he said, ruffling Toby's fur. "You did real good."

Toby wagged his tail, grateful for the praise. He had done his best, and he had proven himself to be a faithful and capable livestock guardian.

The farmer reached into his pocket and pulled out a treat.

Toby's nose twitched and he gobbled it up, his tail wagging in appreciation. He loved treats. And he loved the farmer, who gave him treats and fed him each day and took him to the vet when he needed stitches.

The farmer patted him on the head and then turned toward the truck—his work was calling him.

Toby watched him go, a sense of contentment settling over him as he headed back to his dog shed—his warm bed was calling him.

As Toby Dog walked toward his shed, something about the farmyard seemed off. It was the middle of the day, but it was eerily quiet. Ordinarily, the air would be filled with the sounds of quacking and honking from the ducks and geese. But there was nothing, just the sound of a stiff breeze rattling the bare tree limbs. He looked around. A movement caught his eye.

It was Lil Barn Cat over by the barn. She waved her tail at him, teasing him, and then ducked into the barn.

Tired as he was, he decided he'd best see what that cat was up to.

When Toby stepped into the barn, he was overwhelmed by what he saw. All the animals, the ducks, the geese, the chickens, and even the barn cats, were waiting there to greet him.

Samson was the first to greet him. "Toby Dog, the barn cats told us you fought off the monster that killed my dad."

"I don't think it was a monster," said Toby. "The farmer called it a bobcat. But, yes, I think she was the animal that ate your dad."

"You were so brave," said Jemima. "Thank you, Toby Dog."

"Yes, thank you, Mr. Toby Dog," said Yellow Neck, the drake, sounding uncharacteristically humble. "You have kept my flock safe, and for that, I thank you."

The ducks, geese, and chickens clapped their wings.

Underneath Toby's thick white fur, his cheeks were blushing.

"Oh dude, it looks like quite a party going on here," said a gravelly voice.

Toby turned and saw Grody Otis hiding in the corner.

"Otis! You got away!" yelped Toby Dog.

"I told you that those coyotes are no match for one

of my stinkings. They'll be smelling me for months to come," Otis said and chuckled.

Pablo Barn Cat and Lil Barn Cat glided up to Toby, smiling at him.

"You know, you're really not that bad," said Pablo Barn Cat.

"For a dog, that is," Lil added as she rubbed up against his front legs. "Thanks for saving us, Toby."

"Yeah," said Pablo. "And also, you look like a giant flashlight wearing that silly cone."

Toby chuckled as a tear fell from his eye. His heart swelled with pride as he looked out at the animals gathered around him. He had always known that he was meant to be a guardian, to protect and defend those who couldn't protect themselves. And now, finally, he had proved it. He had saved the farm from the vicious predator that had been terrorizing them, and he had proven himself to be a worthy protector.

As he sat there, surrounded by his friends, Toby knew that he had finally found his home, and he knew that he belonged here. This was where he was meant to be, and he was grateful for every moment he spent here.

Toby closed his eyes and let out a long, contented sigh. He was tired, but he was happy. He was home, and that was all that mattered.

Looking at the animals that surrounded him, Toby's thoughts turned to the future. He knew that there would always be dangers lurking in the shadows, but he also knew that he was ready to face them.

Toby then thought back to when he was just a little puppy still at his mother's farm and how he dreamed of having a farm of his own someday. Looking back on it, he realized that he did not quite know what that meant at the time—how it was both an honor and a responsibility.

Now, sitting here in his crowded dog shed with all the other animals on the farm cheering him on, he knew what it meant. He knew that he had a farm of his very own. He knew that he was Toby Dog of Gold Shaw Farm.

FOLLOW THE REAL-LIFE ADVENTURES OF
GOLD SHAW FARM

Have you fallen in love with Toby Dog, Pablo Barn Cat, Lil Barn Cat, and all our quirky, endearing Gold Shaw Farm friends? The fun doesn't have to stop here! You can join their real-life adventures and become a part of our farm family.

Follow us on YouTube, TikTok, Facebook, and Instagram to stay up to date with our lively crew's antics. There's always something happening at Gold Shaw Farm, and we'd love for you to be a part of it!

@GOLDSHAWFARM

@GOLDSHAWFARM

@GOLDSHAWFARM

@GOLDSHAWFARM

ABOUT THE AUTHOR

Morgan Gold is a farmer and storyteller based in Peacham, Vermont. He raises ducks, geese, chickens, cattle, pigs and trees on his small farm operation. He lives with his wife Allison, two livestock guardian dogs and four barn cats. He is not a cat person.

Made in the USA
Middletown, DE
16 October 2023

40945322R00099